Pooh

JUST BE
NICE
...and not too rough!

By Eleanor Fremont
Illustrated by Darrell Baker

A GOLDEN BOOK • NEW YORK

Golden Books Publishing Company, Inc., New York, New York 10106

Tigger loves to bounce— *boing, boing, boing.*

One day Tigger bounced in to see Pooh, who was just putting away some honey.

"Hul-lo!" said Tigger with a . . .

CRASH!

"Oh, dear," groaned Pooh.

"Sorry, buddy bear," said Tigger. "Want to play?"

"No, thank you, Tigger," Pooh frowned. "I think I'll be stuck here for a while."

"Well, ta-ta for now!" Tigger said.
So off he bounced to Roo's house— boing, boing, boing.
Roo was building a tower of blocks when . . .

CRASH!

"Hey!" shouted Roo.

"Sorry, Roo boy," said Tigger. "Do you want to play?"

"No," answered Roo. "I have to pick up these blocks."

"Okay," Tigger said. "Tally-hoo!" And out he bounced—right into Kanga's washing line.

"Oops!" said Tigger.

"Please, try to be more careful, Tigger," Kanga said.

So Tigger bounced over to see Eeyore, who had just built a nice pile of thistles.

"I don't suppose you've come to play with me, have you?" asked Eeyore.

"Abso-tutely!" said Tigger, bouncing right into Eeyore—and his nice thistle pile.

"I didn't think," Eeyore said, "that a pile of thistles that nice could last long."

Just then Rabbit came along.
"Tigger! Look what you've done!" Rabbit shouted.
"Do you always have to jump on everything?"

"Tiggers don't jump—they bounce!" Tigger answered.
"Well, your bouncing is too rough!" Rabbit scolded.
"So go bounce somewhere else—where you can't
hurt anything!"

"Okay," said Tigger sadly. "I guess no one wants to play with a rough Tigger like me." So off he bounced. It was sort of an unhappy kind of bouncing, though.

Later that day, everyone was having a picnic. Well, almost everyone.

"Where's Tigger?" Piglet asked.

"Off by himself—where he can't hurt anything," Rabbit answered.

"We spent the morning cleaning up Tigger's mess," Kanga said.

"He bounced my thistles, too," said Eeyore.

"And my honey," added Pooh.

"And he trampled my garden just yesterday," Rabbit added. "Something must be done about his roughness!"

"Yes, something," Kanga said.

"Hmmm," wondered Owl.

"Think, think, think!" said Pooh.

In another part of the Hundred-Acre Wood, Tigger was all alone.

"I guess I should get used to being by myself," he said sadly. "Nobody wants to play with a rough Tigger."

Tigger was so busy feeling lonely that he almost
didn't notice Pooh and his friends coming by.

"Are you here to see me?" Tigger asked.

"Yes," answered Pooh. "And we brought you a
present!"

Tigger was so happy, he quickly tore open the gift. "What is it?" he asked.

"It's a Bouncing Thing," said Pooh. "You can bounce on it. Try it!"

So Tigger tried the Bouncing Thing. **Boing, boing, boing,** it went.

"Whoo-hoo! This is the bestest Bouncing Thing ever!" cried Tigger happily. "And Tiggers love to bounce!"

And from then on, Tigger and his friends were much happier. Now that Tigger had a special thing to bounce on, he didn't have to bounce on them anymore.

Well, hardly ever.